Ladybird  Readers

The Unicorn Sleepover

To access the audio and digital versions
of this book:

1 Go to **www.ladybirdeducation.co.uk**
2 Click "Unlock book"
3 Enter the code below

VD4lfelpuT

Notes to teachers, parents, and carers

The *Ladybird Readers* Beginner level helps young language learners to become familiar with key conversational phrases in English. The language introduced has clear real-life applications, giving children the tools to hold their first conversations in English.

This book focuses on simple verbs and provides practice of saying "play", "sing", and "love".

There are some activities to do in this book. They will help children practice these skills:

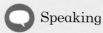 Speaking    Listening*   Writing   Reading   Singing*

*To complete these activities, listen to the audio downloads available at www.ladybirdeducation.co.uk

Series Editor: Sorrel Pitts
Text adapted by Sorrel Pitts
Song lyrics by Fiona Davis

LADYBIRD BOOKS

UK | USA | Canada | Ireland | Australia
India | New Zealand | South Africa

Ladybird Books is part of the Penguin Random House group of companies
whose addresses can be found at global.penguinrandomhouse.com.
www.penguin.co.uk   www.puffin.co.uk   www.ladybird.co.uk

 Penguin
Random House
UK

Text adapted from *My Little Pony* episode "The Traditional Unicorn Sleep-Over" by Hasbro Inc., 2023
This version first published by Ladybird Books, 2023
001

Licensed by:

Printed in China

The authorized representative in the EEA is Penguin Random House Ireland, Morrison Chambers, 32 Nassau Street, Dublin, D02 YH68

A CIP catalogue record for this book is available from the British Library

ISBN: 978-0-241-61689-5

All correspondence to:
Ladybird Books
Penguin Random House Children's
One Embassy Gardens, 8 Viaduct Gardens, London SW11 7BW

FSC
www.fsc.org

MIX
Paper from
responsible sources
FSC® C018179

The Unicorn Sleepover

Based on the *My Little Pony* episode
"The Traditional Unicorn Sleep-Over"

Picture words

 Izzy

 Misty

Unicorn

sleepover

song

Izzy is a Unicorn. She lives in Maretime Bay.

Izzy's friends are not Unicorns.
"I want a Unicorn friend,"
says Izzy.

Then, Izzy meets Misty.

"You are a Unicorn, too!"
says Izzy.

"Please come to my house for a sleepover!" Izzy says. "You can meet my friends!"

"Thank you! I love sleepovers!"
says Misty.

The ponies have their sleepover.

They play games.

They make a lot of food.

"This food is very nice!" says Misty.

Izzy and Misty sing songs.

The ponies talk.

The ponies love their sleepover!

Now, they sleep!

Your turn!

1 **Talk with a friend.** 💬

Where are the ponies?

They are at the sleepover.

What do the ponies do?

They play games and they talk.

2 Listen. Color in the words. 🎧 📖

1 Unicorn   pony

2 friends   games

3 like   love

4 food   song

3 Listen and read. Match. 🎧 📖

1 They play . . .

2 They make a
lot of . . .

3 Izzy and Misty
sing . . .

4 They . . .

4 Listen. Write the first letters.

1  Unicorn

2  Sleepover

3  Song

5 Sing the song.

We play a lot of games.
We meet a new friend.
At Izzy's sleepover.

We make a lot of food.
We sing a lot of songs.
At Izzy's sleepover.

We play and we talk.
We are very good friends.
At Izzy's sleepover.

We love sleepovers!